The Incredible Painting of Felix Clousseau

Jon Agee

Dial Books for Young Readers

Dial Books for Young Readers
An imprint of Penguin Random House LLC, New York

First published in the United States of America by Farrar, Straus and Giroux, 1988
Published by Dial Books for Young Readers, an imprint of Penguin Random House LLC, 2021

Visit us online at penguinrandomhouse.com.

Library of Congress Cataloging-in-Publication Data is available

Printed in China
Dial Books for Young Readers ISBN 9780593112656

10 9 8 7 6 5 4 3 2 1

Design by Cerise Steel
Text set in Clarendon Text Pro

In Paris, the Royal Palace was holding its
Grand Contest of Art. From all over the city,
painters came to show their pictures.

One of them was an unknown painter named Felix Clousseau.

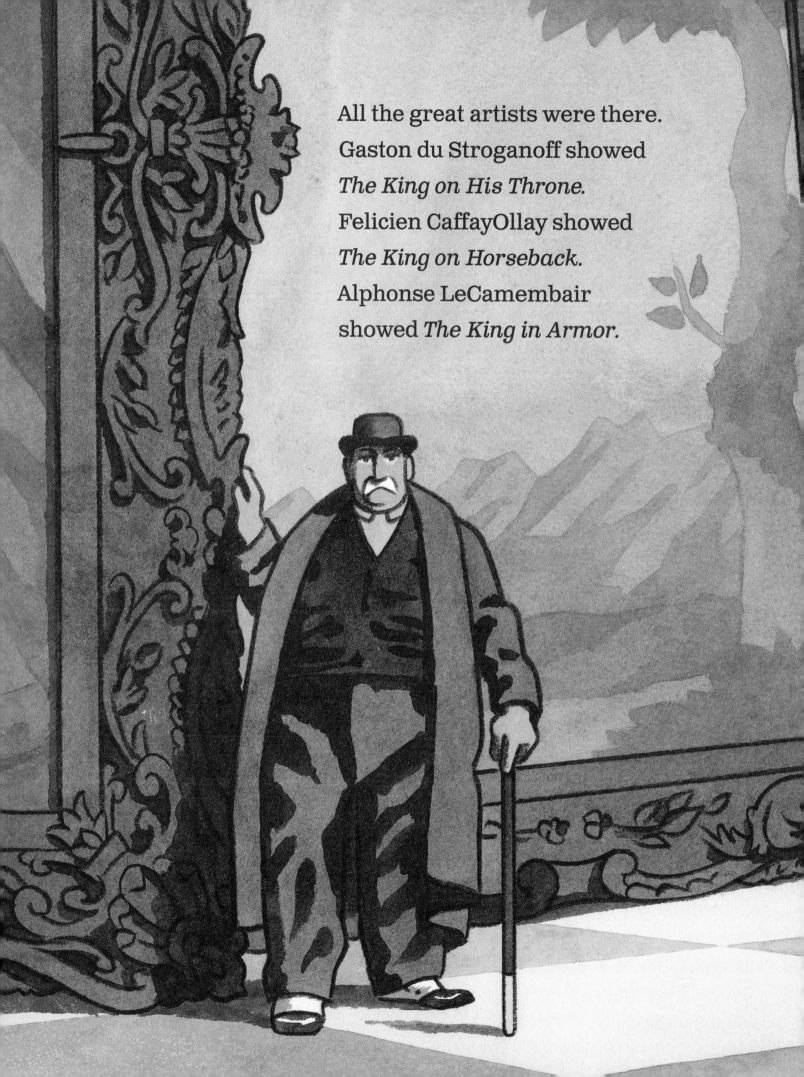

All the great artists were there.
Gaston du Stroganoff showed
The King on His Throne.
Felicien CaffayOllay showed
The King on Horseback.
Alphonse LeCamembair
showed *The King in Armor.*

Then Clousseau showed
his painting.
"Outrageous!" the judges cried.
Never before had they seen
such a ridiculous painting.
Then, suddenly—

—a sound came from the painting.
The judges were stunned.

Clousseau was awarded the Grand Prize.
They called him a genius. It was the first time
in history a painting had quacked.

But that was only half of it.

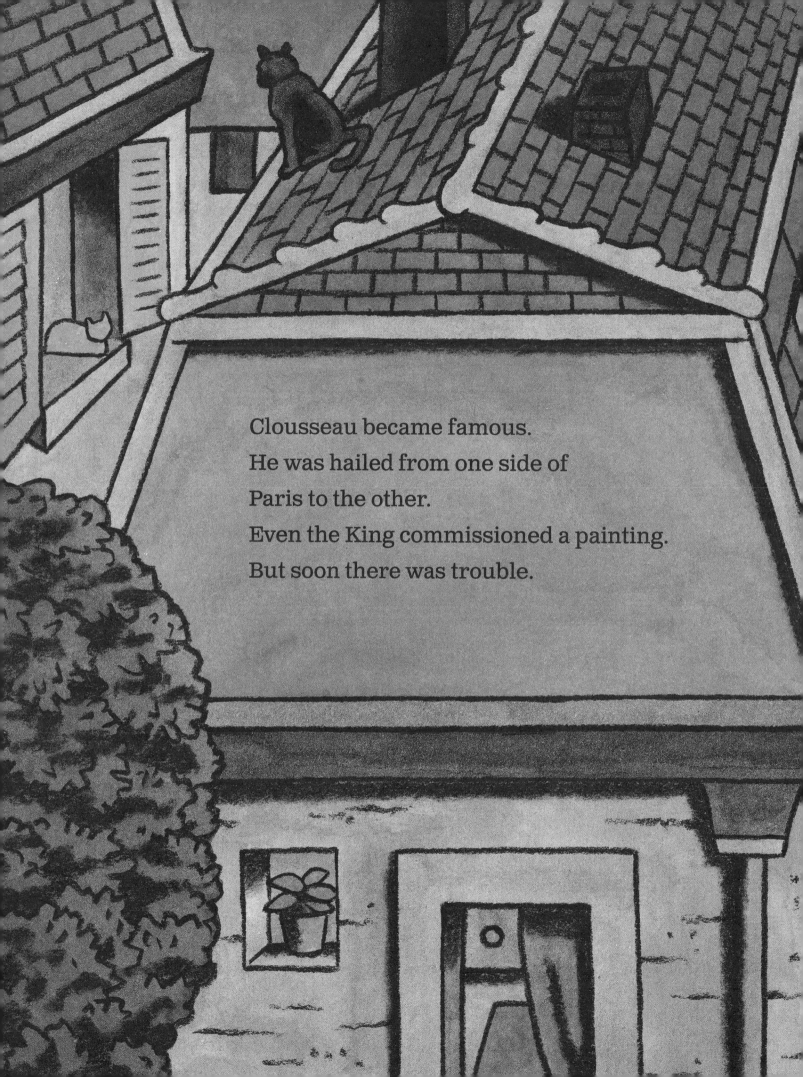

Clousseau became famous.
He was hailed from one side of
Paris to the other.
Even the King commissioned a painting.
But soon there was trouble.

A wealthy baroness owned a Clousseau painting called *The Sleeping Boa Constrictor.* One night, it awoke.

In fact, wherever there was a
Clousseau canvas, there was chaos.

The public was furious!

There were damages! Somebody had to pay!

So Clousseau was sent to prison.

The police gathered up
all of Clousseau's paintings
and put them in a safe place.
All except one.

Meanwhile,
a notorious jewel thief was
on the loose. All over Paris,
diamonds, emeralds, and
sapphires were missing.

One night, the thief broke into the King's Palace to steal the crown.

The next morning,
to the King's surprise, he found the thief—
caught in the grasp of a ferocious dog.
The crown was saved.

Clousseau was a hero.

He was awarded the Medal of Honor.

Released from prison, he went back to his studio...

and returned to his painting.

DATE DUE

BRODART, CO.   Cat. No. 23-221